Voices Are Not for Yelling

Elizabeth Verdick

Illustrated by Marieka Heinlen

free spirit
PUBLISHING®

Library of Congress Cataloging-in-Publication Data
Verdick, Elizabeth.
    Voices are not for yelling / Elizabeth Verdick ; illustrated by Marieka Heinlen.
        pages cm. — (The best behavior series)
    Audience: Ages 4–7.
    ISBN 978-1-57542-501-6 (pbk.) — ISBN 1-57542-501-7 (pbk.) 1. Voice—Juvenile literature. 2. Child psychology—Juvenile literature. I. Heinlen, Marieka, illustrator. II. Title.
    QP306.V47 2015b
    612.7'8—dc23
                                                                                            2014046266

Reading Level Grade 1; Interest Level Ages 4–7;
Fountas & Pinnell Guided Reading Level H

Cover and interior design by Marieka Heinlen

10 9 8 7 6 5 4 3 2 1
Printed in China
R18860115

Free Spirit Publishing Inc.
Minneapolis, MN
(612) 338-2068
help4kids@freespirit.com
www.freespirit.com

Free Spirit offers competitive pricing.
Contact edsales@freespirit.com for pricing information on multiple quantity purchases.

To teachers everywhere,
who make such a big difference
in the lives of little ones.
—E.V.

To my family:
Patrick, Levi, and Nora.
—M.H.

What do you use your voice for?

1

Talking

"Hi!"

2

Asking questions

"How are you?"

Telling jokes

4

Laughing . . .
Ha, ha!

Singing, la, la, la!

You sing high or low, loud or soft,
to fit the feeling of the music.

Your voice is a powerful tool.
How you use it is up to you.

8

You have an indoor
voice that's quiet.

Purrrr

You have an outdoor voice that's LOUD!

Where do you use your indoor voice?

At school, as you work and learn,

or at the
library,

or when
a baby is
asleep.

13

Sometimes, you use your indoor voice in the car or on the bus,

in waiting rooms,

or at the movies.

How does someone ask you to be quiet?

Maybe like this:

zip it, lock it

finger to lips
whispering "Shhh"

peace sign fingers

"Shhh"

slow countdown to 5
(5, 4, 3, 2, 1)

17

Where do you use your outdoor voice?

That's easy . . .

OUTSIDE!

18

A loud voice matches your feelings.

Woof!

You have lots of different feelings.
What happens if you're mad or
frustrated or really, really excited?

Your voice gets louder
and
LOUDER!

But look around you . . .

Are you using your outdoor voice inside?

Because you want to be HEARD?

Voices are not
for yelling.

24

Yelling hurts people's ears— and feelings.

25

Use an indoor voice so people hear the words and not the yelling.

This is how you can quiet your voice:

Take deep breaths in, and then slowly blow them out. In and out, out and in, until your body calms down.

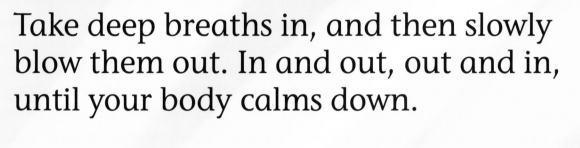

Now it's time to use your words.

"I didn't
mean to.
I'm sorry."

"That's okay. I can build a new one. Will you help me?"

29

Remember, "Voices are not for yelling."

Think before you yell . . . and use your words well!

Tips and Activities for Caregivers and Parents

Using indoor voice versus outdoor voice is a skill all children need to learn, especially when they're in a group setting. Teaching it starts during the toddler years and may continue all the way through elementary school. Here are some ways to introduce, practice, and reinforce this skill.

Indoor/Outdoor Voice

Demonstrate aloud:

- "This is my outdoor voice!" *(loud)*
- "This is my indoor voice." *(normal tone)*
- "This is my quiet voice." *(lower, quieter)*
- "This is my whisper voice." *(whisper)*

Ask the children to try along with you. Give them opportunities for frequent practice during different parts of the day.

Silly vs. Serious

Teach children the differences between "silly time" and "serious time." During silly time, let them be loud with their voices and bodies. Do this outside, if you wish. Show them how to act during serious time, when they need to use a quiet voice and a calm body.

Quiet-Time Gestures

Young children can learn the signs that show it's quiet time. Demonstrate your favorites, and then use them consistently.

Finger to lips

Peace sign fingers

Zip it

lock it

put it in your pocket

Hands up: Teacher raises hand; as soon as each child notices, he or she does the same until everyone has their hand in air.

Countdown from five
You can also teach children a corresponding action to each number:

5	4	3	2	1
Eyes look	Ears listen	Mouth closes	Hands still	Feet quiet

Remember the importance of proximity. If the kids in your care get ramped up, move closer to them. Your presence is a signal that you're paying attention. Now they know you're watching, you hear them, and you're there to step in and help.

Sound Signals

As a caregiver, you probably have your own bag of tricks when it comes to helping children quiet down. Here are a few that are tried-and-true.

"Shhh": When you're shushing children, use a calm, quiet "Shhh" (avoid hissing it loudly).

Clapping: Try a sequence you can repeat, such as two loud claps followed by three rapid ones: *CLAP, CLAP, clap-clap-clap.* Continue until the children settle down.

Or, you might try this sequence:

- "Clap once if you can hear me."
- "Clap twice if you can hear me."
- "Clap three times if you can hear me."

By the time you've reached three claps, most of the children will have quieted down.

"Voices": Teach children that when you say "Voices," their response should be "Shhh." Repeat "Voices" until all the kids are saying "Shhh" and have their eyes on you.

Attention-getters: Purchase an item that makes a special sound that children learn to associate with quieting down. You might choose a bell, a rain stick, a shaker, castanets, or a chime. (Avoid whistles because they're too shrill and are a better option for signaling children outdoors.) Another useful trick is to flick the lights off and on.

"1-2-3, eyes on me": Teach this phrase and use it whenever you need to get the children's attention.

Freeze/Melt: Demonstrate how to freeze in place as soon as the word "Freeze" is said. Then say "Melt," the signal that the children can get back to their work or play.

Ever-quieter voice: A final option is to lower your own voice, getting quieter and quieter until the kids have to listen very closely to hear you. Now you have their attention!

Balanced Classroom

- If kids frequently get wild and revved up in your classroom or group setting, perhaps they need more outdoor time or gross-motor activities.

- Get the kids outside, no matter what the weather. Outdoor time is important for physical, emotional, and social development. Encourage parents to provide weather-appropriate clothing for all occasions (raingear, jackets, hats, and gloves).

- Play quiet classical music when children are restless.

- Have a rest time built into each day. After lunch or outdoor play, create a transitional period where the children can get comfortable on the floor and listen to a quiet story or soft music.

- During group activities when children all want to talk at once, encourage them to raise their hands and take turns. You may wish to use a "talking stick" or "speaking stone" that is passed to the next person whose turn it is.

- Each day, notice when children model appropriate behavior and then reward them with something special: additional free time, a sticker, or the chance to be the classroom helper or leader of the day.

- Sometimes children yell to express strong feelings, such as frustration and anger. You can help by identifying the emotions and showing that you understand. If the yelling persists, you might try: "I'm having trouble hearing you when you yell like that. Please quiet your voice so I can hear you better."

- Practice the "quiet your voice" skill from pages 26–27. You can help children with this skill during heated moments, but even better, teach them ahead of time so they know what to do when their emotions get stirred up. It's easier to call on and reinforce a technique they've already been introduced to.

33

A Word on Yelling

Experts now know that the use of harsh verbal discipline (yelling, swearing, insults) during childhood can have lasting consequences, such as anxiety and depression during the teen and young-adult years. The shouting is remembered long after each occurrence and is hard to forget. Even if parents provide affection as part of their childrearing, the affection does *not* balance out the verbal attacks. The truth is, yelling harms children. There are more effective ways to discipline and guide them.

Children who are frequently yelled at tend to:

- Exhibit worsening behaviors
- Tune out or ignore the person who's yelling
- Yell or become more aggressive at home, at school, and in the community
- Have difficulty learning to manage their feelings and behavior

Parenting isn't easy, and at one time or another we all lose our cool. We yell because our kids do something we don't want them to, or won't do something we've asked them to. In the heat of the moment, we may erupt, but that doesn't mean we can't stop, take a few deep breaths, and apologize. It's never too late to learn a better way.

If you want to provide a more positive atmosphere at home, try some of these ideas:

Post the house rules. Make the rules clear and simple. Phrase them positively (what you expect kids to do) instead of negatively (what they can't do). So, the rules might look like this:

"Use a calm voice."
(Instead of "No yelling!")

"Put toys away after you use them."
(Instead of "Don't leave your junk on the floor.")

State the consequences. What happens in your home if the rules are broken or if children argue or misbehave? Make sure the consequences are age appropriate and have a clear relationship to what occurred.

Offer warnings. You probably know when trouble is brewing—you sense your child's frustration or bad mood, you hear your child getting louder and louder. You might say, "I've asked you once to cooperate with your sister. This is your warning." You can also use *if/then* statements: *"If you grab a toy out of your friend's hands again, then we will end play time early."* Follow through with your warnings.

Use positive reinforcement. Do you find yourself shouting "no" and "don't" too often? Instead of using negative statements, focus on positive ones whenever you can. "I love the way you said *please* and *thank you*." "Wow, you're doing a great job of using your indoor voice!" "I like the way you just told your friend you were sorry." Notice when children do *well*. As parents, we often spend too much time pointing out errors or correcting behavior. Make it a point to watch for times when your child is using an indoor voice, following a rule, or being helpful, and then offer plenty of praise. Children thrive on this kind of positive attention.

Use a firm voice, not a loud one. There are times when children need to know you're serious. Maybe they've broken a rule, hurt someone, or crossed the line. Instead of raising your voice, use a firm tone to tell your child, in simple words, what went wrong and what will happen next. Deliver the message clearly and calmly. (This takes some practice!)

Get down at their level. Communication with young children is more effective when you speak with them face to face at their level. Kneel or sit so you can make good eye contact, which ensures better listening.

Put yourself in their shoes. How do you feel when your spouse, partner, or boss yells at you? Most likely, you get mad, annoyed, frustrated, or upset. You probably want to ignore the person or get away as quickly as possible. Children go through all these emotions when they get yelled at, but they also feel fear. To ensure that your child has a sense of safety and security at home, avoid yelling to express your feelings or to make your child do as you wish. Speak to your child the way you want to be spoken to.

Stay calm. Modeling a calm approach to life is a gift you give your children. They're always watching you for clues and cues on how to act, and if you show them healthy ways to handle frustration and anger, they'll learn how to stay cool in difficult situations. Let them see you take deep breaths to calm down, use a firm voice (instead of yelling), excuse yourself from the room to cool off, and express yourself with poise and equanimity. These are skills they can learn when they're young and use all their lives.

When Yelling Is the Right Thing to Do

There are times when children need to use their voice, words, and body language to tell others "no." Make sure children are aware of "good touch, bad touch" (coming from *anyone*) and "stranger danger." Teach these lessons at home and make sure they are reinforced at school.

Children who practice saying "no" in a loud, strong, clear voice are more likely to stand up for themselves in a situation where someone is hurting them. Practice a loud "no" at home over and over until your child feels comfortable with this. Role-play how to stand up for yourself or get away from someone who is dangerous.

Note: If you suspect that a child is being abused, contact your local Social Services Department, Child Welfare Department, Police Department, or District Attorney's Office. If you teach in a public or private school setting, consult first with your school principal or director to learn the established course of action.

What Children Can Do If There Is Fighting/Yelling at Home

- Think of a safe place to go when the fighting or screaming starts. Make a plan to go to that safe place quickly.

- In that safe place, you can draw, read, or play quietly.

- If you don't feel safe, use a phone to call 911. The person who answers will ask you how they can help. You can tell the person your name and address and say that there is fighting in your home.

- Find a grown-up you trust and talk to that person about the fighting. This person can be a grandparent, an aunt or uncle, a teacher, a neighbor you know well, a caregiver, or a leader at your place of worship. You might say, "There is a lot of yelling and fighting at my home. I'm scared. Can you please help me?"

What Adults Can Do If There Is Verbal Abuse/Fighting at Home

- Call 911.

- Call a local shelter or a domestic abuse hotline.

- Talk with someone you trust who can help: a doctor, a family counselor, a social worker, a therapist, or a religious leader. Your child's school counselor may also be a resource for you. If cost is an issue, it's possible to find low-cost or free services. Keep looking until you find a person or an organization that meets your needs. Enlist the help of trusted relatives and family friends. You need support during this difficult time.

- Stay with friends or relatives while you're getting the help you need.

About the Author and Illustrator

Elizabeth Verdick has been writing books since 1997, the year her daughter was born. Her two children are the inspiration for nearly everything she writes. She is the author of more than 40 highly acclaimed books for children and teens in Free Spirit's Best Behavior®, Toddler Tools®, Happy Healthy Baby®, and Laugh & Learn™ series. Some of her most beloved titles include *Germs Are Not for Sharing, Words Are Not for Hurting, Calm-Down Time, Don't Behave Like You Live in a Cave, Stand Up to Bullying!,* and *The Survival Guide for Kids with Autism Spectrum Disorders (And Their Parents).* She lives with her husband, two children, and a houseful of pets near St. Paul, Minnesota.

Marieka Heinlen received her BFA at the University of Wisconsin, Madison, and also studied at Central Saint Martins College of Art and Design in London. She launched her career as an award-winning children's book illustrator with *Hands Are Not for Hitting* and has illustrated all of the books in the Best Behavior and Toddler Tools series. Marieka focuses her work on books and other materials for children, teens, parents, and teachers. She lives in St. Paul, Minnesota, with her husband, son, and daughter.

Best Behavior® English-Spanish Editions

Paperback
Ages 4–7

Board Book
Ages 0–3

Paperback
Ages 4–7

Board Book
Ages 0–3

Paperback
Ages 4–7

Board Book
Ages 0–3

Board Book
Ages 0–3